Bootie

The Schoolboy

MIKE JAMES

Text copyright © Mike James 2011
ISBN: 9781921787379
Published by Vivid Publishing
P.O. Box 948, Fremantle
Western Australia 6959
www.vividpublishing.com.au

Chapters

1

The Letter

There aren't many better ways to spend your summer holidays than at the beach. One good thing about Bootsie's family moving last year was that they now lived very close to the beach, and Bootsie loved it. Bootsie and Robbie had become very good friends during Bootsie's first season with the Hornets and although the boys only made the quarterfinals they were still pleased with their own efforts. Both boys loved the beach and most days they would ride their bikes down and swim in the ocean after going for a run along the sand.

If they weren't at the beach there was always the river. Bootsie, Robbie and some other boys who lived close by had made a rope swing on a large tree branch that hung out over the water. Each of the boys would take turns to swing from the river bank and let go of the rope when it swung out over the deeper water making a huge splash as they hit the water. They met a boy down the river who they nicknamed 'Daredevil Dan' his real name was Danny but he was the only boy who would jump from the branch where the rope was tied from and into the water. It was a huge drop into the water and the boys thought he was crazy to do it.

Dan soon became friends with both Bootsie and Robbie. His dad was a police officer and he ran the local boxing club. For some extra fitness over the summer, Bootsie and Robbie would go to the boxing club and meet up with Dan. Dan's dad had been training boxers for many years, he was a good boxer when he was younger and had been a golden gloves champion himself. Dan loved to box as well which was good because his dad loved to train him. All that Dan talked about was going to the Olympic Games as a boxer and winning a gold medal.

Some mornings the three boys would go for a jog together. Dan ran every morning and didn't miss a day, he was really into his boxing which was just as well because his touch rugby skills were pretty bad. The boys played in a team on Monday nights and Dan would always be dropping the ball. No one would dare say anything because all the boys knew how good he was at boxing. Bootsie and Robbie would do some sparring against Dan but he would always take it a bit easy on the two of them. Dan's dad used to put Dan in the ring with much older boys. His dad said it was good for him to train against the older boys. When Bootsie saw Dan get a really bad blood nose from a punch from a much older boy, he knew boxing wasn't the sport for him. Sure Bootsie had been hit and hurt in tackles but he still thought rugby was far better than boxing. He did like the extra fitness training that it gave him though.

Robbie had the same ideas about it as Bootsie. "There's no way I'm getting my face squashed like that," Robbie said to Bootsie on the way home from the gym that day.

"Poor Dan, that boy was pretty big he was sparring today. That punch would have really hurt him," replied Bootsie.

"Yep he's going to be good but end up with the face of a forward," Robbie laughed.

"What does that mean?" questioned Bootsie.

"You know the fly-halfs get the girls cause were the good looking ones," replied Robbie.

"That's because you get fed the ball and don't have to dive into the rucks"

Bootsie joked back. "The forwards win the game and the backs decide by how much."

"No way. It's all about the backs," replied Robbie quickly.

"Well I can tell you one thing, we're never going to agree on this one," said Bootsie.

"Yeah that's for sure," replied Robbie.

Bootsie said goodbye to Robbie as they walked past Robbie's house, "See you tomorrow then Robbie," said Bootsie as he continued to his house.

"Yep last day of holidays we'd better make it a good one," replied Robbie.

Bootsie went inside and grabbed a drink from the fridge.

"How was your day?" His mum asked as he sat down.

"Good, we went to the gym and watched Dan spar some of the older boys," he replied.

"I'm glad I don't have to watch you

box, I think rugby is rough enough for you," his mum said to him.

"You've got no worries about me Mum, I'll never stop playing rugby for boxing that's for sure," replied Bootsie.

"Speaking about rugby there's a letter for you, I think it's got to do with rugby, I've seen that logo on the envelope before," his mum told Bootsie.

Bootsie looked at the letter; there was a blue shield on the top left hand corner with a maroon cross in the middle of it. He opened the envelope and read the letter to his mum.

Dear Selected Student,
Congratulations you have been invited to train for selection in the regional schoolboys' rugby competition. A camp will be held early into the new season where 75 boys from each age group will train and a 22 boy side will be selected from each age group

to represent the region in this year's Regional Schoolboys Cup Competition. You will receive a further letter, which will inform you of times, dates and what you will need to bring to the camp.

If you have any questions or feel at this stage you cannot make it to the selection camp or choose not to take part in the camp, please contact the regional rugby office on the telephone numbers below. If you are interested in attending the selection camp you need to contact the offices in the next 30 days after receiving this letter.

Once again congratulations on your initial selection.

President: Northern Region Rugby Union.

"Oh Bootsie that is fantastic," his mum said as he finished reading the letter out loud to her.

"Wow," replied Bootsie, "I don't know what to say," he added. "Can I go and show coach?" he asked his mum.

"Sure you can he will be so proud of you for this."

Bootsie grabbed his bike and started riding towards the coach's house near the small park at the end of his street. As he rode past Robbie's house Robbie came flying out of his driveway on his bike.

"Robbie," Bootsie shouted. "Where are you going?"

"Um to show coach something," Robbie replied.

"It's not a letter is it?" he asked Robbie.

"Did you?" Robbie asked Bootsie excitedly.

"Yep, I got one too," said Bootsie with a huge smile on his face. "Let's go together and show him." The boys agreed.

"I can't believe we're going to the regional schoolboys' camp together Bootsie," said Robbie.

"Yep, this could be the start of a great year," Bootsie replied.

2

Northern Region

Rugby Union

Meliora Cogito

1882

Whatever it Takes

The boys were so excited when they arrived at their former coach's house that they forgot one thing, 'Tank'.

"Hi Becky" a startled Bootsie said when she answered the door.

"Hi" she replied.

"Um is your dad home?" Bootsie asked.

"Yeah I'll get him for you if you want, come in and wait for him," Becky replied.

The boys walked into the living room of the coach's house.

"Becky" Robbie said to Bootsie with a smile.

"Yeah she told me last year during a game, I was as shocked as you are, I didn't even think about her being here when we tell him," continued Bootsie.

"It's pretty unfair that she can't play anymore and we're here telling her dad about our letters," replied Robbie.

"Maybe we should go," said Bootsie.

"Go where?" the coach asked as he entered the living room.

"Nowhere, its ok," replied Robbie.

"How are you boys, had a good summer?" he asked.

"Good coach, we're good," they replied.

"Now what did you want to see me about?" he asked them both.

"We wanted to show you our letters but we forgot about..," said Bootsie.

"Forgot about what?" asked the coach.

"Um," Robbie muttered as he tried to help Bootsie.

"They forgot about me," said Becky as she entered the room. "Don't worry boys I saw the shield on the envelopes of your letters, I know what they are. Really its fine I'm really pleased for you both," she added.

The boys handed the coach their letters, he moved his glasses to the end of his nose and read the letters to himself. He finished reading and looked at the boys. "Come with me" he said as he led the boys down a hallway of the house and into his study. "Have a look around" he said to the boys. The walls of the study were covered with framed photos of the coach playing rugby. There were club photos, regional team photos and many test team photos. There were also a number of framed jumpers on the walls as well. He led the boys over to one particular jumper which was framed and hanging on the wall. The boys knew straight away what the jumper was. They both stared at the maroon, dark blue and light blue jumper in the frame. Bootsie noticed the shield on the top left of the jumper.

"Hey that's the same shield that's on the envelope and the bottom of the letter," he said to the coach.

"Got it in one Bootsie. You boys know what it means to wear this jumper don't you?" the coach asked them.

"Yep sure do," they replied.

"This was my first regional jumper," said the coach as he looked at the jumper on the wall.

"This one means as much to me as any of the test jumpers over there," he added as he pointed to a collection of framed test match jumpers on another wall. The boys stared around the room in awe of what the coach was showing them.

"It all starts right here," continued the coach, "Pride for your region, the northern region. This is only a letter so far boys, you haven't got to wear one of these jumpers yet. There will be plenty of lads trying to get hold of

one of these and stop you from getting one instead of them. Remember
what I have always told you boys, do
whatever it takes to get into the team
and when you're in that team, to stay
in the team. This could be a step-
ping stone to that," the coach paused
and pointed to a particular jumper on
the far wall. "Do you know what this
jumper is?" he asked.
"Yes, it's a test jumper," replied
Bootsie.
"Yes, it is a test jumper, but it's *the*
jumper I wore in a winning world cup
match," the coach told both boys, as
they stood there staring at it with their
mouths wide open.

He slowly walked them out to the front
of his house.
"It's good that you boys have been
given the chance to attend the camp,
but it's only the first step of many
to come. No one will give you that

jumper if you don't earn it. There are plenty of good players in this region and each one of them wants to wear one as much as you two do. You boys are going to have to fight to wear one of them, ok?" He said as they walked up the driveway together.

"I'm sure your new coach this season will tell you the same things that I have today, have you met him yet?" asked the coach.

"Not yet, we've got three weeks left of the touch season and then preseason starts. I guess we'll meet him then" replied Bootsie.

"You boys did very well last season especially to get picked on one quarter final appearance. Normally only boys from the semi and grand final games get selected, so you must have impressed someone watching," the coach said.

"Don't forget, contenders from all over the region will be there, a lot of them you would have never played against before. Just be prepared for anything when you get there. Even at your young age it's going to be very competitive, that's about all I can tell you both," the coach told the boys. "Oh and don't worry about 'Tank' she knew she could never play regional rugby as a junior. Hopefully one day she'll play for the region in the senior women's competition. I know I'll be helping coach the team if she does," he smiled.

The boys said goodbye. They both knew that he was probably the best coach that they had living in the town and it was a shame that he didn't want to continue to coach now his daughter wasn't allowed to play anymore. Bootsie was keen to get home and tell his dad about the letter as he would be home from work soon. As they neared Robbie's house, Robbie stopped Bootsie and said to him, "Ever since I was six years old I've wanted one of those jumpers. I know you want one too, whatever it takes, let's make sure that we both get one. Ok? I'll help you, and you help me."

Bootsie looked at Robbie, "Definitely, whatever it takes, this year we will both get one together. I promise," Bootsie replied. The boys shook hands and said as one, "Whatever it takes, whatever it takes."

3

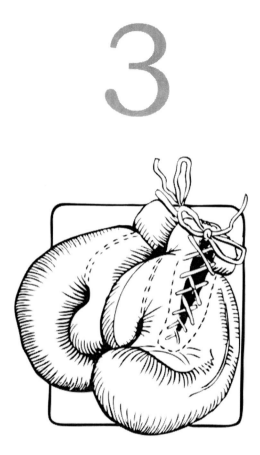

New Season,
New Coach

Bootsie finished his touch rugby season off with a win. The team he played in had finished 5th out of 18 teams, which he didn't think was too bad. He mainly used the competition to keep fit over summer. For Bootsie his real passion was for the tackling game and he couldn't wait for the first night of preseason training. He did think to himself that last year at this time he also couldn't wait for preseason to begin and ended up crying his eyes out at the end of the night.

"What a year," he thought to himself as he sat in the front seat of his dad's car on the way home from touch.

"I wouldn't mind playing a bit of touch next year," his dad said to him.

"Really?" Bootsie asked.

"Yeah it looks like a bit of fun and a good social thing to do," his dad continued.

"At least it's on a Monday night and you don't have to work late," added Bootsie.

"Oh well maybe next year," his dad replied.

Bootsie had a week's break before preseason training began, he started going to the park down the road again with Robbie to do some sprint training and ball skills. Robbie spent most of the time place kicking for goals. He would throw his kicking tee across the grass and wherever it landed he would kick the ball from there. If he missed the goal he would stay at that spot until he got it over the crossbar. He didn't miss too many.

"How'd you get so good at that?" asked Bootsie.

"Practice," replied Robbie. "I've been coming down to these posts since I was about five and trying to do this. I used to use a little mini rugby ball and stand on the five metre line until I could get it over the crossbar. When I could, I started to move back a bit and then out a bit until I just got better at it," he answered. "Coach used to tell me last year no team will win a game if the fly half is weak. You're the playmaker and without a good kicker the team is weak," Robbie said to Bootsie. "It's like I said Bootsie, it's all about the backs," he added.

"Don't start that again," Bootsie replied.

The boys also went down to the boxing club to train a few nights before the Wednesday evening that preseason started. Dan was preparing for his first year of competition in the golden gloves tournament. He was a good boxer and both boys had to try really hard just to keep up with him. It was very different training than for rugby. Dan's dad was a very hard trainer and had no time for lazy people in his gym. Lucky for Bootsie and Robbie, because their focus was getting fit for the upcoming schoolboy's camp, so being lazy was not a problem for either of them.

"Why would you want to get punched in the head for a sport?" Robbie asked Bootsie.

"I don't know, I think it's pretty good," replied Bootsie. "You've got to be pretty tough to make it in this game" he added.

"Yeah you end up with a squashed up face and ugly," said Robbie. "Ugly like a forward?" asked Bootsie.

"No, not that ugly," laughed Robbie, as he started to move around like a boxer in a fight. Dan's dad saw Robbie dancing around like a boxer. "Look at him move, do you want to get in the ring and do a few rounds with Dan?" asked Dan's dad.

"Oh no thanks, not today," replied Robbie.

"He said he doesn't want to get ugly like a boxer," Bootsie added, to spice things up. Some of the other boys heard Bootsie's comment and stopped punching the bags.

"I was err just, you know kidding," Robbie said as he started to back pedal out of his comment. The other boys started to punch the bags again.

"Thanks Bootsie," snapped Robbie. "You nearly got me flattened." "What, flattened like a forward?" Bootsie joked. Both boys looked around and started to laugh.

"Enough laughing, you two either train or leave," Dan's dad shouted to the boys. Bootsie and Robbie finished the session both still sniggering about their near miss.

Preseason training finally came and Bootsie was very excited to begin a new season. His dad still worked late on Wednesday evenings which meant he still had to ride his bike to training each week. He convinced Robbie to join him to help strengthen his leg muscles as well. Robbie had lived here since he was born and had no trouble getting up the hills. He was only a bit slower than Bootsie, but at least he could get up the hills the first night of preseason, not like Bootsie the year before.

The boys arrived at the ground and rode over to where they usually trained. There were the usual familiar faces like Brains, Sidestep, Dozer, Horse, Ferret, Legs and Flash, but there were also a lot of new faces as well. One new face was a boy who quickly earned the nickname 'Rhino', he was a very short boy but what he lacked in height he made up for in size. He was one very solid boy and a funny thing was that he appeared to have no neck at all; his head looked like it just sat on his very, very wide shoulders. Bootsie was very pleased when Rhino said he only played hooker, because this year Bootsie wanted his old, number 8 position back and he would leave Matty and Rhino to compete for the number 2 jumper. Bootsie again thought about what the coach had said last year. "No heart, no commitment."

There was also a new coach; he introduced himself to the boys as Mr Butkiss.
"Hello boys and welcome to the first night of training," he said as he introduced himself. "I moved here over summer with my family and I

am looking forward to being your new coach. This is my son Chris and he is playing his first season of rugby this year," continued the coach.

"Oh great," Bootsie thought to himself.

"Now I have been coaching soccer lately but seeing that it's not played around here we are going to try rugby this year," he added.

"He could try netball," Robbie whispered to Bootsie. Bootsie laughed out loud at Robbie's comment. This made everyone look at Bootsie including his new coach.

"Ok then, sport is all about fun and I want each of you to have fun this season. Each week we will take turns at who gets a game so it's fair for everyone. It's not about winning or losing, it's all about fun," continued Mr Butkiss.

"Oh man, take turns, have fun," Bootsie thought to himself. "I know it's about fun but it is nice to win as well," he also thought. Bootsie and Robbie just looked at each other.

"Regional schoolboys, let's just concentrate on regional schoolboys," said Bootsie.

"I agree," replied Robbie.

The boys had a very different start to the first night of preseason than either of them had ever had before. Firstly they had a tug of war competition, which was a lot of fun, and at one point it was five boys against Rhino, who was on his own and they still couldn't move him. He was one strong boy. They then moved onto 100 metre sprint races, which then turned into 100 metre baton relay races. Bootsie just thought about what the coach had said last year. "No heart, no commitment. We'll see how many come back if they don't get a game," he thought to himself. They also played a game, but with red ribbons hanging from the back of their shorts and instead of tackling you had to pull the ribbon out of the shorts to stop a player. Bootsie and Robbie just used it as a fitness run and it worked. Even *they* were exhausted after it. The game was so fast it was hard to keep up. None of the players from last year had said anything to them about receiving a letter and they didn't want to go around telling everyone that they had received one.

"No one likes a bragger," Bootsie's dad always said to him, so Bootsie and Robbie kept it to themselves. That was until Ferret asked and the secret was out. The boys from last year's team were very happy for the both of them and none of them said anything negative about the selection letters.

When Bootsie arrived home his dad was sitting outside drinking a beer. "How was it?" he asked.

"Different," replied Bootsie.

"What's your new coach like?" asked his dad.

"Different," replied Bootsie. "Very different," he added as he walked into the house.

4

"Different, Very Different"

The following Wednesday the boys arrived at training and again Mr Butkiss had some very different ideas. Firstly the boys had a tug of war competition which was a lot of fun at least. Then they moved onto 100 metre sprint races, which then turned into 100 metre baton relay races. Once again the boys played a game of rugby using the ribbons. Bootsie and Robbie wanted to get fit for the schoolboy camp and under Mr Butkiss it was working. The new coach didn't just watch, he took part in every aspect of the games, from racing in the 100 metre sprints to being anchor man on the end of the tug of war rope. It was a completely different start to a season than any of the boys had had under previous coaches. It was very different from last season especially for Bootsie who was told, if you can't keep up you can't play. This year it was, if you can't keep up I'll help you keep up.

Considering the new coach's son had never played rugby before, he was a quick learner. He was an extremely fast runner and very fit. He thrashed Mirrors in his 100 metre race and just beat Flash in his race. Chris was very good with the rugby ball as well; he had no problems passing or catching and was very good at finding gaps in the defence, he was a natural. During the ribbon game he scored three tries for Bootsie's team. Ferret wanted to know why he wasn't going to the schoolboys camp if he could score three tries and Bootsie and Robbie didn't get any. Mr Butkiss pulled Bootsie and Robbie aside at the half time break at training.
"I was told that you boys were chosen to go to the regional trials camp and I

wanted to let you know that I'm behind you 100 percent. If I can do anything to help you, just let me know ok?" he said to the two boys.

Bootsie was shocked by the friendly attitude of the new coach and his coaching methods, he thought about Coach Van Den who was a good coach but could get very grumpy, very quickly too. Last year's coach was a test legend but he was a very hard man.
"Mr Butkiss is the total opposite of both of them, he is friendly, helpful and runs around with us. Different, very different," he said to himself.

For the second half of training that evening the coach put a ribbon hanging out of the shorts at the back of one boy and the boy who chased him had to pull it out before he got to the end of the 100 metre line. The boy in front was given a 10 metre start which really made the boy chasing run extra hard. Most of the boys were really struggling to keep up with the pace of the session.

"Fitness boys, that's how we'll beat them, with superior fitness," the coach said to his boys. Another thing the new coach did was he always kept the ball wet; he had a bucket full of water that he regularly threw the ball in. He also put some washing detergent in there, which really made the ball slippery as well.

"Anyone can catch a dry ball. Where's the challenge in that?" he said to the boys who spent most of the night dropping a slimy ball.

Another thing the new coach taught the boys were passing drills. He had players coming in at all angles to take passes and fool the defence. His son Chris said that his dad stayed up all night watching old games and drawing pictures of plays. There were also names for each of the different plays. Most of the boys knew the scissors move, where the ball is quickly passed and the two players cross like a pair of scissors closing. These moves were very different to even that. There were lots of quick passes and dummy runners going all over the place. It all took place with the greasy ball as well, which was still being dropped at most plays. Mr Butkiss never got angry at any player once, he was very patient with the boys and took time with each boy separately, to help him in whatever he was having trouble with, especially the new passing drills.

Bootsie was shocked when Mr Butkiss told him he was way too slow when he was coming off the defensive line.
"Don't hold back and wait for them to run at you, once their halfback pulls the ball out of the back of a ruck or

scrum and passes it, that's when you need to run at *them* and catch *them* off guard. If you give the other team room to play the ball they will, and you'll be missing a great opportunity to shut down their passing play. Just make sure you're behind the last feet of *your* players on *your* side of the ruck and you won't be penalised for being offside either," he said to Bootsie.

"Oh ok," was all that Bootsie replied. "What do you know about rugby? You're just a soccer coach," he said to himself as the coach walked away.

The coach pulled Robbie aside and told him to keep his head up more and be aware of what his players were doing and when he spotted a hole in the defensive wall to put his player through it. Robbie walked over to Bootsie and said, "This man thinks he knows everything about rugby but he's never coached a rugby team before, I'm not listening to him." Bootsie didn't know what to say, it was alright to think it to himself but he didn't want to criticize the coach to other people. His dad always said to him, "Don't be so quick to knock new things before you've really given them a go." He thought about what the coach had said and thought maybe he should listen to new ideas.

Robbie really had a hard time when the coach tried to help him with his goal kicking.
"Anyone can kick a round ball," Robbie snapped at him at one point. "Robbie I'm not criticizing you, I'm just saying that it will help your kicking if you follow through with your kicking leg when you kick," Mr Butkiss explained to a very angry Robbie. Bootsie couldn't believe that he was so calm after Robbie got so angry at him. Bootsie went over to Chris.
"Is your dad always so calm, like this?" Bootsie asked.

"Oh yes he never gets too angry. I mean if you did something wrong towards him he would, but he hardly ever raises his voice," replied Chris.

"Hey Bootsie," said Chris as he called Bootsie back. "He really is a good coach. In time you'll see how good he is," continued Chris.

"I just hope Robbie listens to him then," replied Bootsie.

After training Bootsie looked around for Robbie but he couldn't find him anywhere. He noticed his bike was gone and when he asked Ferret where Robbie was, he said that he had already left and was not very happy either. Bootsie rode home alone and thought about what the new coach had said to him and to Robbie.

"Don't knock it till you try it," he kept saying to himself. "I didn't want to come here and dad said why don't you at least give it a go first and now I love this place." Bootsie decided he would give the coach a chance. What did he have to lose anyway?

5

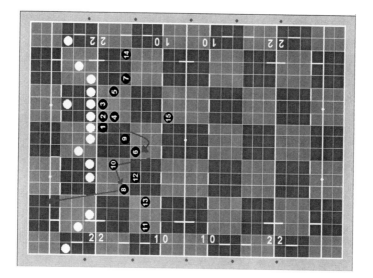

Magnets

The first game of the new season, Bootsie couldn't believe how fast the previous year had gone. "Another season starts today," his mum said to him with a smile at the breakfast table that morning.

"Yeah it's come around again already," replied Bootsie.

"How is the team looking this year?" his dad asked.

"It's just so different at training so far, we play soccer, do tugs of war, 100 metre sprints and rugby with ribbons instead of tackling most nights. I'm not sure he knows what he's doing," replied Bootsie. "Our new coach is nice but he has some very different methods than last year's coach or coach Van Den," added Bootsie. "I want the hornets to do well but I can't stop thinking about the schoolboy camp coming up," he said to his dad. "Well don't forget where you came from," replied his dad.

"What does that mean?" asked a confused Bootsie.

"You can't forget about your club just because you might get to play regional rugby this year. If you don't make it and believe me I hope you do, the club will still be there for you and your new coach," replied his dad. "If you don't like the coach, well life's like that, you can't like or get on with everybody. But if you don't listen to him or think you know it all then he might ask you not to play after the schoolboy camp and then you're really in trouble," added his dad.

Bootsie knew his dad was right, again. He decided he would listen and really try to do what his new coach asked of him, Robbie thought the opposite. Bootsie arrived at the ground and looked for Mr Butkiss and the others, but Mr Butkiss found him and his family instead.

"Hello Bootsie and parents," he said in his jovial voice. "I'm John Butkiss, Bootsie's coach this year," he said as he shook hands with Bootsie's mum and dad.

"Ready for the big game Bootsie?" he asked.

"Yeah I sure am," replied Bootsie.

"Well the rest of the players are over there so go and join them and I'll be over shortly," he added.

Bootsie walked over and left Mr Butkiss talking with his parents. When he arrived at the group he noticed a large board with a green rugby field marked out on it. There were white and black magnets with numbers written on them to represent the players on the field. Mr Butkiss soon joined the players and began to speak to the group.

"Ok boys and welcome to our first game of the season. Now this board will be our play board for the year so get used to it. When you get your jumper have a look at the board. When I show you what plays I want, I want you to look at the board and see where your number comes into it. As I said, it's all about fun so let's enjoy ourselves today. If you don't play today then you will play next week and if you play today you might not play next week depending on player numbers. I will try to be as fair as I can all year but we do have a lot of players but not enough to have two teams in the competition," he said to the group.

"If it's like last year we'll have 22 players at training on Wednesday again and that will be it for the season," Bootsie said to Robbie.

"I wish it was last year and we had a real coach coaching this team. We are going to get smashed out there today," replied Robbie.

"I think you might be right," thought Bootsie to himself. "Let's just give it our best," he said to Robbie.

Mr Butkiss read out the names of the boys playing today and both Bootsie and Robbie got to play.

"It's starting better than last season anyway," Bootsie thought to himself. "This time last year I was on the bench and didn't even get to play.

At least this season I'm playing and I've got the number 8 jumper," he said to Robbie as they took the field.

What a great team to play first up, last year's grand final winners, the Central Cobras. Bootsie wasn't surprised when the Cobras scored within five minutes of the opening half. With a successful conversion, the score was

Cobras 7, Hornets 0. The boys tried some of the passing plays that they had worked on at training, but they weren't successful at all. Either the boys would miss the passes or end up blocking the player with the ball and give away a penalty for obstruction. With the amount of penalties given away and the amazing boot on the Cobra's flyhalf the halftime score was Cobras 15, Hornets 0.

"It's ok boys, I've seen some positive things out there, don't worry about the score it's not important at this end of the season," said Mr Butkiss to the boys at half time.
"The plays will come don't worry about that, when a team plays together for the first time and they're trying new things it's bound to take time to sort it out. I want you to try just one simple move. By the time the opposition

works it out we should have scored at least two or three tries and we'll be back in this game. Now everyone look at the board," continued the coach.

The coach moved the magnets around and showed the boys the one simple move he wanted them to do.
"Ok boys look at your number on these magnets and follow what you have to do. When we get inside their 22 and we get in a good ruck position or a scrum this is what I want." He moved the magnets around and showed each boy what he wanted him to do.
"Ok Robbie, it all comes down to you when you switch the play to Ferret there and he comes back inside he will pass the ball back to Bootsie, who will dummy and pass straight back to you, a huge gap will open here and boom you flick it straight back to Bootsie and he's through easy. Do this at the breakdown or from a scrum and we'll

get two or three tries before they can work it out," continued the coach. "Ok good luck and believe in yourselves," he added.

"Another coach telling me to believe in myself, I do and I know it works," Bootsie laughed to Robbie.
"Breakdown, what does he know about a breakdown? He probably thinks it's when your car breaks down on the side of the road. He can take his magnets home as well. What a waste of time they are!" replied an angry Robbie.

The second half started and again the Cobras were on the board in the first 5 minutes.
"Bootsie get up on their line quicker, you're allowing them to play the ball too much," Mr Butkiss shouted to Bootsie. After the conversion the score was Cobras 22, Hornets 0. One thing Bootsie *did* notice was the

Cobras were really slowing down and the Hornets were still at the same level. When the ball came out of a scrum or ruck Bootsie charged at the defence quicker and it was stopping them from getting the ball out to the backs. At one ruck he was so quick and hard at the ball, he knocked it clear from the tackled player, picked it up and crossed the line for one of the easiest tries he had ever scored.

"It works," he said to himself, "It really works." With the successful kick the score was Cobras 22, Hornets 7.

Amazingly Mr Butkiss's son Chris scored a length of the field try from a lazy intercept pass and no Cobras' player got within 40 metres of him. Even the referee was struggling to keep up with him; he was well outside the 22 metre line when Chris scored. Just in case you didn't know, if a referee can't keep up with a fast running player and he's outside the 22 metre area when the try is scored, it's called *'joining the 22 metre club'*. The crowd definitely let the referee know *he* had joined the 22 metre club that day. After the kick, the score was a respectable Cobras 22, Hornets 14.

With a minute to go, the ball was just outside the Cobras' 22 metre line. "The magnets," Bootsie shouted, "Do the magnets move," he shouted again. The ball came out and Robbie switched the play to Ferret, he came back inside and passed to Bootsie. Bootsie did a quick run and dummy and flicked it back to Robbie, Bootsie couldn't believe the huge gap that opened up in front of him.

"Pass!" he screamed to Robbie. Robbie ignored Bootsie and went for the line himself only to be met by a sea of defenders who would have all missed Bootsie completely. Smash!! Robbie got hit and hit hard holding the ball. He dropped the ball and a Cobras player dived on it. The referee blew his whistle and said it was full time. Final score Cobras 22, Hornets 14.

Bootsie was devastated. Robbie's attitude had got in the way and he should have scored. He shook hands with all the Cobras who looked exhausted. Bootsie was surprised, and felt like he could play another half.

"Good game boys," said coach Butkiss, "we'll make them plays work next time."

Bootsie was amazed how relaxed Mr Butkiss was, who must have known what Robbie had done. He must have known his plan had worked and he still was happy with the boys, even Robbie. Bootsie just couldn't understand it. On the way home he realized they had taken it up to the Cobras and if he'd scored, they would have only lost by a point to last year's grand final winners. Maybe Mr Butkiss really did know his stuff. It was too bad that Robbie couldn't see it.

6

"Meliora Cogito"

When Bootsie arrived home from school on Monday he knew something was up just by the look on his Mum's face.

"What's wrong?" he asked her.

"Oh' nothing. Why?" she replied.

"I can tell, that's why," he said.

"Oh' ok then," she said excitedly, as she reached for something on top of the fridge. "I wanted to wait until your dad got home for you to open it, but here do it now, I can't wait any longer," she replied as she handed Bootsie an envelope. Just by the shield on the corner of the envelope he knew this was what he was waiting for.

"Yes!" he said excitedly as he opened the envelope.

Dear Selected Student,
As per the previous letter and your phonecall stating your desire to attend the northern region schoolboys 4 day

rugby camp, we would like to inform you that the camp will begin on Friday the 28th of this month. You will need to arrive at camp after 5pm on Thursday the 27th of this month to prepare for a Friday morning start to selection.

You will need to bring such items as your own boots, protective clothing, mouth guard and all toiletries. If successful you will be provided with a regional team tracksuit, team shorts, socks and a new pair of boots.

We look forward to seeing you at camp and good luck with your attempt for selection.

President: Northern Region Rugby Union.

"This Thursday! I have to be there this Thursday!!" said Bootsie.

"Let me see the envelope," his mum said, "Look this was stamped on the 2nd of this month. I wonder why it has taken so long to get here," she continued.

"That means I miss two days of school. Cool." replied Bootsie. "Doesn't give us much time to get you ready though, does it?" answered his mum. Bootsie ran out of the house with his letter, and ran down to Robbie's house. He met Robbie who had just opened his letter, while standing by the mailbox.

"Bootsie we're going to camp this week," he said excitedly, "Finally some decent coaching," he added, Bootsie was not happy about the last comment Robbie made. He decided not to say anything.

Wednesday afternoon Bootsie started to get ready for training.

"Bootsie we need to go and get your stuff and get you ready for tomorrow," his mum said. "You'll have to miss training tonight," she added.

"Miss training, but I've never missed training," he said.

"Yes and you've never been selected for a schoolboy camp either," his mum quickly answered back. "You need to be packed and ready tonight so we can leave just after 4pm tomorrow afternoon," she added.

"What do I need to get?" asked Bootsie.

"Toiletries. Soap, toothpaste, shampoo and anything else you may need. We'll go to the shops now and get you packed when we get back," she continued.

Bootsie was disappointed about missing training but realized that he was getting ready for his first school-boy camp. As he lay in bed that night and looked at the posters of Test players on his walls, he realized that one day in the past, they too would have gone to their first camp. If Bootsie wanted this so much, why was he so nervous?

After he arrived home from school on Thursday, Bootsie was a very excited boy.

"Camp, I'm going to camp," was all he kept saying. He sat looking out of the front window of the house waiting for his dad to arrive home from work. When he saw the car pull into the driveway he grabbed his suitcase and ran outside.

"Can we go now?" he asked his dad excitedly.

"Yes of course, just let me go inside and grab a drink first, ok?" replied his dad.

Bootsie's mum had arranged for Robbie to go to the camp in their car with Bootsie and his family. They drove down to the camp, which was about an hour away from their home. They arrived just after 5pm just like it said in the letter. There were a lot of boys arriving at the same time as Bootsie and the boys realized that they only knew each other. There were 75 boys selected from each age group with 2 coaches for each team. The boys had to go and sign a registration form to say that they had arrived. Bootsie and Robbie were so pleased to see their names on the board as they signed in.

After about an hour, Bootsie's mum and dad said they would be leaving the boys, to go home. It suddenly dawned on Bootsie he had never been away from his parents and home before. He felt very worried about it, but didn't want to show it in front of his parents and Robbie. A man on a megaphone was saying he wanted all the boys inside the hall immediately, so Bootsie had to hurry and say goodbye quickly.

"We'll see you on Monday afternoon," his mum said as she hugged Bootsie. "Good luck son," said his dad as he rubbed him on the top of his head. Bootsie and Robbie made their way into the hall after they watched Bootsie's parents drive away.

With so many boys in such a large hall it was very loud indeed.

"Ok listen up," a huge man bellowed to the boys from the stage. "HEY!!" he shouted in order to quiet the group down. "OK, thank you," he said. "Now boys, you all know why you're here, if you don't maybe you should leave now," said the man as all the boys laughed. "Have a look around you at the plaques and photos of boys and men who have been here before you. Look at the shield on the wall there," he said, as he pointed to a massive shield on the wall, the same one that was on the envelope and letter Bootsie had received. "Meliora Cogito," he shouted. "I strive for the best, that's what it means. Remember it, never forget it. I strive for the best," he said again. "That's what's expected of you if you want to play for this region. To do what these great men and boys on the walls have gone before you and done. It's not just a jumper or a game, it's about pride and passion, passion for that jumper and that shield. 1882!!" he shouted loudly. "Since 1882 that's how long men have worn these colours. That's how long it's been since this great region started to play this great game, and you boys are the future. How bad do you want it? Well we'll find out over the next few days won't we!!" The man walked off the stage to a huge round of applause. If he was there to fire up the boys he had succeeded, for the rest of the evening every boy was talking about winning a jumper for himself and nothing else.

After dinner Bootsie left the dining room he walked around the hall, where the man had given his speech earlier. He looked at the plaques on the wall and the photos of players from the past. There were framed jumpers on the wall and one of them was an original jumper worn in the first game in 1882. Bootsie found many pictures of his previous coach whose name was also on the life members plaque. He was quite a hero within these walls. As he stood and looked at the life member plaque, the huge man who had given the speech came and stood next to him.

"Heroes," he said to Bootsie. "Each and every one of them a hero, son," he said again.

"He was my coach last year," said Bootsie as he pointed to the coach's name on the board.

"WELL!!" the man said loudly. "What a great man, one of the finest players to wear these colours ever," he continued. "A legend among legends," he added. "Son, one day you might wake up and realize what you missed out on if you don't get to wear these colours," he said as he looked down at Bootsie. "Don't let it happen to you, do you understand me?" he asked Bootsie.

Bootsie looked up at the huge man and said, "Don't worry I'm going to do whatever it takes to make the team."

The man looked at Bootsie and went silent for a good minute. Bootsie was very worried he had offended the man.

"Such wise words from someone so young," he said to Bootsie. The man took Bootsie's hand in his and said, "Good luck young man, with that attitude you deserve to wear these great colours." Bootsie was so pleased hearing this. He didn't know this man was also a legendry player for the region and at one time he had been the coach of Bootsie's coach last year. It was him who had taught Bootsie's coach that saying.

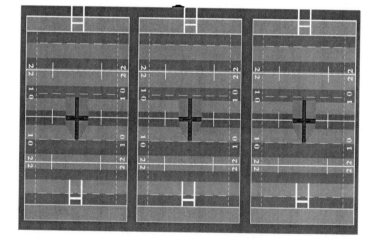

Camp

Very early the next morning the boys at camp were woken for breakfast. This was all very new for Bootsie, not the being up early, but having so many boys around at once. It was a queue for everything like showers, toilets and food. After breakfast in the dining hall the boys were split into their age groups and taken to different grounds. The camp was situated on what used to be an army barracks, which was no longer used by the army and was bought by the Regional Rugby Union Board. It had a massive dining hall and plenty of dormitories for the boys to sleep. Outside, it had three full-size rugby fields all in a line next to each other. Bootsie walked down to the oval with the other boys from his age group. When they arrived, there were two men waiting on the oval for them. Bootsie knew one of the men was a current Test player who played flyhalf and he knew that the other man was an ex Test player who had retired not too long ago.

After the men introduced themselves, the boys were split into two groups, the forwards and the backs. Bootsie's group was coached by the ex Test player, who was also the main coach. All morning they practiced lineouts, scrums, mauls and Bootsie's favourite, rucks! Bootsie loved flying into rucks and clearing players who were on their feet, away from the ball.

After Bootsie explained to the coaches that he felt more comfortable playing number 8 rather than hooker he was placed into every back row position in the scrum, but when he was put into the number 8 spot he really shone. He loved to pick the ball up from the back of the scrum and charge at the defence and although he had played hooker for the first time with the Hornets, he knew it wasn't a natural position for him and number 8 was where he was best. He made some really good breaks off the back of the scrum, but each time he broke the defensive line he was called back and the scrum was reset.

The boys stopped for lunch and were allowed to rest until late into the afternoon. Bootsie fell asleep for a few hours after what was a very hard morning session. The afternoon session was pretty much the same as the morning but with extra lineout work. Bootsie had very sore arms from lifting the lineout jumpers all evening in the second session. They practiced driving mauls from the lineout over and over again. By the end of the second session Bootsie was exhausted, he had dinner and like most of the other boys went straight to bed. There were a few boys making plenty of noise still, but Bootsie was so tired he had no problems drifting off to sleep.

Early Saturday morning was the same as the previous day, the boys were split into two groups and did separate sessions. All morning it was scrum practice with the scrum machine. Scrum after scrum was set and reset. One thing Bootsie did notice was that he was number 8 all morning, some of the other boys were still being rotated, but he stayed at the back of the scrum, which didn't bother him at all. After lunch they were allowed another rest until another hard session a bit later in the evening. It was a furious pace but Bootsie felt he had the fitness level to keep up. The coach brought out tackle bags and for most of the evening Bootsie and the rest of the forwards had to tackle these bags. The coach didn't let the boys rest at all; this was a real step up in training for all the boys. Again that night Bootsie was so exhausted he was struggling to stay awake even at the dinner table. It wasn't long after dinner that he was in bed and asleep.

Sunday morning was just the same as the previous mornings, early start with no let up in the toughness of training. This morning the group was split into two teams with both the forwards and the backs combining together to form two full teams. Bootsie and Robbie were on the same team which they both liked. Bootsie was shocked and excited at the same time when he noticed the other team's flyhalf was Ben 'Super Boot' Smith from the Bulldogs. He gave him a quick wave but Ben didn't wave back. The game started and it wasn't long before Bootsie was in the thick of the action.

His extra training and the new fitness training from Mr Butkiss had really helped him out a lot. He ran and ran all through the game and made sure he got to every breakdown as quick as possible to help out the tackled player. He knew this was the job of a good forward. Bootsie also loved the contact and was never afraid to hold onto the ball and charge into the defensive line of the other team always trying to gain ground for his team, another job of the forwards.

During one ruck, Bootsie was standing in the defensive line waiting for the other team's halfback to pass the ball out to the first receiver, who just happened to be Ben 'Super Boot' Smith. Bootsie took Mr Butkiss' advice and charged at Ben when he received the pass. Before he could get boot to ball, Bootsie was up on him and crunched him. Unfortunately for Ben he lost the ball forwards and Bootsie's team turned it into a try. During the game players were being switched between teams and had to swap the red and blue bibs with numbers on them between each other. Pretty soon Bootsie's team started to really dominate the game, their scrum absolutely smashed the other scrum each time it was set. Bootsie came off the back of the scrum with the ball and pushed off three players before he was brought down in a tackle.

At the end of the game Bootsie ran over to Ben.

"Ben, it's me Bootsie," said Bootsie.

"Bootsie?" replied a shocked Ben, "How did you get so big?"

"Extra training and Mum's bacon and eggs I suppose," Bootsie replied.

"Look at your legs, they're huge!" said Ben.

"All the hills where I live now," replied Bootsie.

The boys sat next to each other at lunch and talked about old times and the Bulldogs. They had a new coach last year and another new coach this year. Last year they finished just out of the top teams and didn't make the finals but had won most of their games so far this year. Bootsie was really pleased to speak with him.

"Do you think you'll make the team?" Bootsie asked him.

"No way, that boy there will get the flyhalf spot," replied Ben pointing at another boy.

"That's Robbie; he's on my team, The Hornets. I didn't even think that's who you would be competing against for your spot," said Bootsie. "He's really good Ben, don't feel bad if you miss out on it to him," Bootsie said to Ben.

The evening session was quite easy compared to the morning session that day. The two teams that played together in the morning were separated again and the whole team went through set piece plays. They would set a scrum and feed the ball out through either the halfback passing it out, or Bootsie would have to pick it up and run off the back of the scrum with it. After you ran with the ball the coach would shout "Ok tackled," and the player with the ball had to go to ground and place the ball out. The forwards had to drive over like it was a real ruck and protect the ball. Then the halfback would come in and pass the ball out and the same would happen again and again. The coach continually shouted, "Remember, if you're not on your feet then you're not part of the game."

Bootsie knew this was a good time to impress so he made every effort to get to each ruck and protect the tackled player and knock the defending player trying to grab the ball off his feet. By the end of the session he was exhausted, he had never run so much at training before, never.

The boys were told as a group to head back to the showers and be in the dining hall within an hour for dinner. Bootsie wanted to run back to the showers to finally be first and get a hot one, but he was too exhausted and could only walk back in front of the coaches. He had dinner and went straight to bed; he knew the following morning's session was the most important one and the last chance to impress the coaches.

When Bootsie woke the following morning he knew it was much later in the morning than when they were usually woken up.

"Did I sleep in?" he asked one of the coaches he saw near the dining room.

"No we let you sleep in on the last day; we'd made our choice for the team by Sunday night. After breakfast the teams will be announced," replied the coach. Bootsie panicked, "Did I do enough to impress the coaches?" he said to himself. After breakfast the boys had to assemble in the main hall again. There was a huge pile of maroon and blue tracksuits on one of the tables and another table full of orange boxes with brand new blue boots in them. The big man once again took the stage.

"Well done to all of you for participating in the camp and giving it everything you had. Only 22 players from each group will be selected. If your name is read out please stand up and come up onto the stage behind me.

The man started to read from a list, Bootsie's age group was first. One by one each boy would get up and move to the stage when his name was called out. Suddenly Bootsie realised something, every boy that was on his team was going up onto the stage, and then it happened; Bootsie's name was read out at number 8 followed the halfback at 9 and then Robbie at number 10. Bootsie couldn't believe it; he had been selected for his age group and Robbie had made it too. He was beaming as he stood on the stage and shook hands with the huge man once again. Once all the teams had been read out, the selected players were given their regional rugby tracksuits, shorts, socks and a brand new pair of blue boots.

Bootsie packed his bag and put on his new tracksuit to wear home. When his parents drove towards the boys they could see they were both wearing the regional tracksuits. Bootsie's mum and dad jumped out of the car.

"You boys made it," said Bootie's mum as she hugged Robbie and Bootsie together.

"Well done boys," said his dad as he joined the hug.

On the way home Robbie looked at Bootsie and said, "One of the coaches told me I can kick well but I'm stubborn, can you believe that?" Bootsie just turned, looked out the window and thought to himself, "Yes Robbie, you sure are."

8

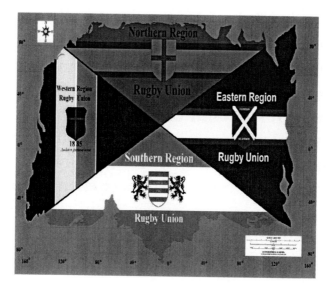

Regional Rugby

The Wednesday after Bootsie had received his regional selection he and his parents were invited to a huge dinner at a large hotel in the city. It was for the region's top grade senior players to be given their jumpers for the first game on Saturday. All the successful players no matter what age were invited to the dinner. For Bootsie and Robbie it was a huge event, with so many players that Bootsie had seen on TV and on the posters in his bedroom he nearly filled his autograph book. The same huge man from the camp gave a speech before each player came onto the stage to be handed his jumper. It was a great night and Bootsie couldn't wait to play in that jumper on Saturday.

Finally Saturday morning came and Bootsie got to wear his new tracksuit again. He packed his rugby bag double-checking he had his scrum cap, boots and mouth guard. His parents had to drive him to a bus that was waiting in a car park not too far from their house. He said goodbye to his parents, who said they would see him at the game. As the bus drove away, he waved to his parents through the windows of the bus. The game was being played at the same ground the big match would be played on later in the night. Bootsie's game was the first one in the morning and then each schoolboy age group would play until the big first grade clash later that evening. The change rooms the boys used were painted in the colours of the northern region's team colours, dark blue, light blue and maroon. This was a lot bigger than his grand final game with the Bulldogs; Bootsie had similar nerves though and remembered that coach Van Den said it was all normal.

He got dressed in his gear and his jumper was laid out on a table with all the other boy's jumpers. From the moment he put it on it felt special, like he had superpowers. He felt so proud to be wearing a jumper he had watched his idols wear on TV so often before. His coach was the ex Test player from the camp who had also played for the region when he was younger. He gave a speech about pride and passion for the jumper and what it meant to represent your region. The last thing he said to the group before they went onto the field made Bootsie smile, he looked at the boys and said, "The forwards are going to win the game and the backs will decide by how much." When he said it, Bootsie looked over at Robbie and smiled. Robbie didn't smile back, he looked sick!!

When they ran out onto the ground, Bootsie was in shock at how big the stadium looked. He had been here before to watch big matches but had never seen it from the ground before and he imagined what it might be like to play later that night when it was packed with fans screaming and shouting. At the moment it was pretty much just the parents of the boys in the team watching and it was very empty. Bootsie couldn't stop thinking to himself, "I'm playing for my region; I'm playing for my region," as he stood on the field waiting. The Western Region's colours were red, yellow and black. They had a black shield with a blue cross in the middle of their jumper with the words, "Audaces fortuna iuvat" written under it in Latin, it meant "Fortune favours the bold". They were also a proud rugby region and had started playing in 1885. The referee blew his whistle and the game was on.

Right from the opening whistle it was tough, Bootsie was running and tackling then chasing again, more tackling more running and finally the ball went out of play so he could stop to catch his breath. If the game went like this for the whole match he wasn't sure if he could make it to the end. He felt like he had used up half his energy levels in the first ten minutes. At the first scrum of the game he was sucking in huge deep breaths of air before it was set. This was a great chance for the forwards to stamp their authority on the game. The scrum packed down and Bootsie pushed from behind as hard as he could. His team's halfback put the ball in and it was soon under Bootsie's feet, he was careful to keep control of the ball until the halfback made it around to the back of the scrum to take it out and pass it out to Robbie as first receiver. Robbie passed it on to the inside centre who found a gap and was through. He was tackled on the 22 metre line and Bootsie was the first forward to help clean out the defenders and protect the ball.

The ball was recycled quickly and he was constantly running to the breakdowns for support. The forwards kept up the pressure and it was telling on the other team, pretty soon the ball was on the Western Region's 5 metre line. Bootsie picked up the ball and drove for the line but was stopped; he placed the ball back for the next forward to drive over and protect the ball. The halfback picked it up, dummy passed and dived through the gap when the defenders on the line fell for it. Robbie got his first points for his region with an easy conversion, Northern Region 7 and Western Region 0.

The game was ferocious, there were a lot of injured players leaving the field with cuts and bumps. Bootsie made it through the entire first half and had made some great tackles. At half time the score was still Northern Region 7, Western Region 0.

At the half time break the coach really shouted at Robbie to stop trying to kick drop goals, he had tried to kick three and had missed each time. Robbie had told Bootsie earlier in the week he was going to kick a drop goal for his region in one of the next two matches no matter what. The coach really shouted at the team, "Remember this year we're playing for the Regional Cup, if we lose today's game we're out. We only get one chance and that's this game. Losing this week isn't an option, do you hear me?" he said in no uncertain terms. After the coach's spray towards Robbie, Bootsie wasn't so sure about the drop goal idea anymore. The halftime break was over and they were soon in the thick of the action again.

Bootsie kept running and running. He felt better in the second half and had controlled his breathing to conserve his energy. Nerves at the start of a game can really make your breath heavy and use up a lot of energy. It had happened to Bootsie in the first half and he wasn't going to let it happen in the second half. He was always quick off the line to punish the defenders. He still couldn't believe a soccer coach had taught him this each time he tackled a player and slowed their play down. The northern region team was a very good mix of players but they had one problem, discipline. Some of the boys kept putting their hands in the ruck even after the referee called out, "Ruck!" this caused two penalties. Another boy was then penalized for not entering the ruck from behind the last feet of the players forming the ruck.

"In from the side," the referee said after he blew his whistle. All three penalties resulted in shots at the goals and each was successful, the western region team was now ahead 9-7. This game was important but Bootsie and the others knew they were the better team and favourites to win. If they could win this and the other favoured region won their game in the other match it would set up a clash next week between the two biggest rival regions, northern and southern. Last year in the first grade game they had played each other in the first match and Bootsie's region had been knocked out of the playing for the cup because of that first game. Before Bootsie's team could worry about next week they had to win this game first.

Time was slowly ticking by and the western region was still in front by 2 points. Bootsie said to Robbie to try the magnet play that Mr Butkiss had taught them, Robbie laughed at him and told him that he shouldn't listen to what Mr Butkiss had told him. Bootsie got really mad at Robbie; however he was nowhere near as mad as his coach when Robbie tried for another drop goal and missed. Robbie was soon replaced for another reserve player. The other team now had a 22 metre drop out; the ball was kicked high and luckily gathered by Bootsie's team. The player that caught the ball ran and gained his team some good ground. They quickly recycled the ball and were gaining some good territory, Bootsie continually ran hard into the rucks to clean out the defending players who were on their feet and trying to grab the ball.

When one of the western region's players went down injured, Bootsie grabbed the reserve flyhalf and the halfback and explained the magnet play to them. They agreed that at the next breakdown to use it, the ball was going to be quickly passed and then passed back again, Bootsie would dummy the defence and when the gap opened up 'Boom' he was going to pass and it would be try time. The referee had already said this was the last play of the game when the injured player got to his feet.

They packed down the scrum and the ball was soon under Bootsie's feet. As the ball was picked up by the halfback Bootsie shouted to him, "At the next ruck set up the magnet play." The halfback flew in grabbed the ball and said, "Yep," and was out again following the ball. He threw a long cut out pass to the inside centre totally freeing up the flyhalf for the magnet move. When Bootsie saw this he knew the move was on. The inside centre did his job and took the ball into the tackle and went straight to ground. The halfback was straight in there and got the ball out to the running flyhalf, he quickly passed back to the halfback who quickly passed to Bootsie. Bootsie did a quick run and dummy and 'Boom' a huge gap opened. He fed the ball to the running flyhalf who went straight through the gap and in for the try. Bootsie was so pleased it had worked, the halfback and the flyhalf jumped all over Bootsie after the try was scored and he didn't even score it.

"I wish Mr Butkiss could have seen that," he said to himself.

After the conversion the siren sounded and the referee blew the final whistle. The final score was Northern Region 14, Western Region 9. Bootsie's coach was so pleased the boys had won, in fact all but one of northern region teams won that day including the senior team later in the evening. Bootsie and his family were given free tickets to that game and in front of thousands and thousands of people got to watch the top game and his region win. It set up a huge game the following week for the senior team and Bootsie's team against their region's biggest and oldest rivals. Northern V Southern.

9

Southern Region

Acta non verba
1882

Rugby Union

Action Not Words

Robbie's dad drove the boys to regional training on Wednesday evening and Bootsie was very quiet. He was still quite mad at Robbie for his attitude towards Mr Butkiss and now to make things worse he wasn't listening to the regional coach either. He had been replaced for trying to kick a drop goal for himself. It wasn't what was best for the team, it was purely selfish because he wanted to say he had kicked a drop goal for his region. Bootsie wasn't the only one with this opinion and when they arrived at training Robbie was taken aside by the assistant coach and given extra training for his lack of discipline in the last game. After he was so exhausted he couldn't run anymore and in front of the group he was also informed he was starting the next game on the bench. It was his turn to be the quiet one on the way home from training.

The boys travelled to the southern region by a large bus on Friday and stayed at a large base that was once used as a prison. The former prison had a massive dining hall just like at the regional camp. Bootsie wasn't too comfortable about sleeping in an old cell. He was very pleased to have a choice of either fruit and cereal or bacon and eggs for breakfast in the morning; he chose the bacon and eggs. The boys were driven to the stadium on Saturday morning in plenty of time to get changed for the game. That's the first and last time I'll see the inside of a prison he thought to himself as they departed from the prison and headed for the stadium. That night was the big grudge match between the two biggest rival regions, Northern V Southern. The Southern team had made short work of the Eastern Region the previous week and the Northern Region had had little trouble with the Western Region. This stadium would be completely full for tonight's game, but for Bootsie's game, it was again very empty.

The team got changed in the visitors change room, someone had put up heaps of maroon, and blue ribbons so the northern teams would feel somewhat at home. But they knew they were in hostile opposition territory, this was a red and white region. The Southern Region's colours were red and white striped jumpers, white shorts with red and white striped socks. Their motto in Latin said "Acta non verba" which meant 'action not words'. They wore their colours with as much pride as the Northern Region wore their own colours of maroon tops with light blue sections down the sides and on the shoulders with small dark blue stripes in the light blue sections.

Maroon shorts with light and dark blue stripes down the side and maroon and light blue striped socks with the top section that gets folded over being dark blue. These were the two biggest regions and the teams had played their first game against each other in 1882, so it was a huge rivalry between the two regions. The games between these two regions always pulled the biggest crowds whenever they were in the final together.

Bootsie was feeling a little tense before the game and he knew the sound of the opening whistle would ease the nerves. It couldn't come soon enough for him, "Pheew," the referee blew his whistle and the game was on. The new starting flyhalf for Bootsie's team kicked off and sent the ball high and deep into the Southern Region's half. The forwards did a good job to chase after the kick and stop the

Southern attackers in their own half. The Southern team was a lot better opposition than the Western Region the previous Saturday. The Southern Region was like the Northern Region, purely a rugby region. They took the game very seriously and it showed by the talents of their players. The Northern Region team was on the back foot early and with constant attacking play the Southern Region was on the board early with a pretty easy under the posts try. First score Southern Region 7, Northern Region 0.

The Northern's flyhalf was instructed to put up plenty of big kicks and put the opposition under pressure from the high ball; at least he did what he was told. After a barrage of high bombs the fullback finally dropped one and because of the knock on the Northern team got the scrum feed inside the Southern team's 22. Bootsie loved playing number 8; he loved it at the back of the scrum, really using his powerful legs to drive the scrum. Pretty soon the ball was under his feet, the scrum pushed forwards and Bootsie rolled the ball along with his feet. He was careful to keep control of the ball and not let it out of the scrum, this way the opposition halfback had to have both his feet behind the ball or he would be penalised for offside. The scrum push gained some good territory and when the halfback passed it out they were deep inside the 22 metre zone. The halfback shouted, "Magnet" and the move from last week was tried again, this time however the Southern Region didn't fall for Bootsie's dummy pass and he got flattened. He went to ground and hung onto the ball, he heard the referee shout, "Let it go."

"Where are my forwards?" Bootsie thought to himself knowing what was coming.

"Pheew," the referee blew his whistle. "Penalty against number 8 for not releasing," said the referee. Bootsie knew he had done it and quickly got back ten metres, he had given away one penalty he didn't want to give away one for not retreating ten metres. The Southern team player took a quick tap kick and ran past Bootsie, Bootsie knew he wasn't back the full ten metres yet, so he couldn't touch him and had to let him run past him. The quick kick had taken the northern players by surprise and the Southern team quickly passed it out wide and was now inside the Northern team's half.

Bootsie knew his team had been in a good attacking position and with him giving away a penalty it had now resulted in the Southern Region pushing their way towards the Northern goal line. He ran back and defended hard, there was no way he was going to let this result in a try to the other team. The ball was soon on the northern five metre line and all the Northern players were spread out on their goal line furiously defending the line. The Southern team picked up the ball and drove at the line but time after time the Northern defence was up to the challenge and pushed them back each time. Soon enough they lost the ball forward and when the Northern team won the scrum and the ball was booted up field and over the touch line the pressure was off, Bootsie was the most relieved player that's for sure. The game was very tight and after one of the Northern players gave away a penalty for offside when they were inside their own 22, the score at half time was Southern 10, Northern 0.

At the half time break the coach was pretty calm with the boys, "Glimpses of brilliance and glimpses of stupidity, that's what I've seen so far," he said to the group. "Watch the discipline again," he said as he looked at Bootsie. "Where was the support for Bootsie when we were on their five metre line?" he asked the boys. "What's he supposed to do?" he asked.

Suddenly the coach's voice changed and he began to shout at the team to fire the boys up.
"Get out there and support your players, get right up into the opposition's faces, out do what they can do. I want 100 percent from all of you and I'm only seeing it from half of you. I want a better second

half effort," he said and then told the group to get back out onto the field. Bootsie was just pleased he didn't get a spray for the penalty and got out of the change room quickly.

It started to rain heavily at the start of the second half and the southern region's colours were soon mud brown and red. It was funny when they would put on a replacement player and his clothes looked so clean when he ran out onto the field ready for action. The rain made the game very scrappy and Bootsie liked it this way, he had played in very wet games before and he knew exactly what to do, hang onto the ball! Each time he got the ball he ignored the passes and drove into the defence, it worked for him but the other players who passed the ball had no luck catching the wet ball and there were a lot of knock-ons which resulted in a lot of turnovers.

It wouldn't have been a very good game to watch with the number of dropped balls and scrums taking place. When a Southern player lost the ball forwards after a dropped pass, it rolled towards Bootsie's foot, so he just booted the ball up field and took off after it. One of his backs overtook him and picked up the ball as he ran towards the try line but was soon tackled. As he went down, he quickly passed the ball to Bootsie. The pass was terrible and was thrown at about sock height. Bootsie had to lean very far forward to even get his hands close to the ball. He got his fingertips to the wet ball but could feel he didn't have hold of the slippery ball properly. In a split-second flash he remembered the ball in the bucket of water and detergent that Mr Butkiss made them practice with at Hornets training, this is what this ball felt like. The extra practice with the slippery ball helped Bootsie keep control and he dived over the line, grounding the slippery pill for a try. He was mobbed by his players. After the conversion the score was Southern 10, Northern 7.

It was getting very late into the game and Robbie came onto the field in his very clean clothes when the starting flyhalf went off injured. Bootsie knew they needed a try to win and no drop goal would win this today. "A draw is good but a win is better," he thought to himself. The Southern players were being careful to not give away any penalties and make the game a possible draw. The Northern team had good possession and with no time left was making good ground deep into the southern half of the field. The forwards were doing good work driving the ball up the field. Robbie kept screaming for the pass and since he kept dropping back, Bootsie was very worried about his drop goal comment last week and each time Bootsie had the ball he ignored Robbie completely. The siren went and the pressure was now on, the boys knew as soon as they lost possession the game was over.

The halfback passed out and put a player under so much pressure he was forced to pass to Robbie. Bootsie looked on in horror as Robbie set himself for the drop goal, the other team's players shouted, "Drop goal" and they froze to watch the ball take flight. Robbie faked the kick and ran towards the line; he had caught all the defensive players off guard and went straight through a gap to score. Even Bootsie was slow to realize what he had just done; he thought for sure the drop goal was on. Robbie converted his own try and the final score was Southern 10, Northern 14.

"Actions not words," Robbie said to Bootsie as they hugged after the game. It was a start of new things to come, all the northern region teams won that day including a win for the senior team later that evening. As for Robbie his selfish attitude had been changed forever before the start of that game, he had realized there was no *I* in the word team.

THE DAILY NEWS

THE REGIONS FINEST NEWSPAPER

Butkiss Sacked as Coach

Coach of the Northern Region first grade team was sacked last night after crashing out of the Regional Shield after losing all three of their games and ending the Northern Regions campaign this time around. Butkiss who himself is a former Regional player whose career was tragically cut short in his prime due to a knee injury stated at a press conference last night said he was immediately informed of the board's decision to stand him down. He stated the injury toll his team had taken before and during the Shield Competition had not helped his cause. President of the Northern Region Rugby Board said it would be impossible for Butkiss to continue in the head coach role next season in the Regional Cup Competition. "This Regional Shield Competition only comes around every four years and for the Northern Region to finish last is unacceptable" the President of the Northern Board said at the same press conference after the game last night. Butkiss was seen to leave the stadium before his players after he addressed them in the changing rooms shortly after the press conference to inform them he had been stood down as coach.

The True Hero

At School on Monday morning Bootsie and Robbie were awarded a special certificate from the Regional Rugby Union Board, which was given to them at an assembly. They shook hands with the school principal and stood beside her as she told the rest of the school about what Bootsie and Robbie had achieved in the last few weeks. A girl from the school who had been selected and had played for the regional netball team over the previous two weekends was also was given a certificate.

Bootsie couldn't wait to get back to Hornets training on Wednesday afternoon and see all his team mates. Robbie came to Bootsie's house very early as he was in a particular hurry to get to training himself. Robbie had realized his mistake and wanted to speak to Mr Butkiss about his attitude and that he had now realized he was wrong to doubt his coaching ability. When the boys arrived at training they couldn't believe how many boys were still there. Normally the numbers started to drop off the longer the season went on, but this season there were still as many boys now as there were at the start of the season. Robbie went and spoke to Mr Butkiss while Bootsie caught up with the rest of the boys that he hadn't seen since the regional camp had begun all those weeks ago. Mr Butkiss was very kind to Robbie and told him it was fine and there was always a spot in the team for him.

As he walked with Robbie, Mr Butkiss told him he just wanted to show him one thing before they rejoined the rest of the team. He grabbed a kicking tee and they headed for the ten metre line, not the one closet to the goal but the ten metre line on the other side of the halfway line. Mr Butkiss set a rugby ball on top of the kicking tee.

"Now Robbie I am going to do this twice and I want you to watch my foot very closely," he said to Robbie. "The first time I am going to put my support foot about where you put yours which is just a bit too far away from the tee, just watch what happens," he added as he started to walk backwards away from the tee. Mr Butkiss started his approach to the kick and "Woomf!!!" he booted the ball which had the distance but it hooked badly and missed the goal by a mile.

"Ok now this time I'm going to kick like I want you to kick," he explained to Robbie who was very interested in the demonstration. He again positioned the ball on the tee; the ball was 60 metres away from the goal posts mind you. He took some steps backwards to position himself for the kick, then made his approach to the ball and "Woomf" the ball travelled high, long, dead straight and easily cleared the crossbar.

"What was the difference?" he asked Robbie.

"Your support leg wasn't as close to the tee and you followed through with your kicking leg," replied Robbie. "I already know it works, when I was at camp I got to work with the current test flyhalf and he told me the same thing." added Robbie.

"I know Robbie. He told me," replied the coach to a stunned Robbie. "How did he tell you?" he asked his coach.

"He rang me after the camp and we got to talking about the boys at camp and your name came up. I used to be his coach at one time when he was a junior player. We are still good friends and speak quite often, he also told me about the drop goals and the replacement in your first game. I was very pleased to hear how you turned a bad situation into a positive a week later though Robbie. It shows the makings of a great player to do that, it showed maturity." he said to a very stunned Robbie.

Robbie was now Mr Butkiss's biggest supporter and never doubted his methods again no matter how far out of the box they seemed. Bootsie had learned a few things whilst he spoke with the rest of the players as well. The Hornets had won every game since he and Robbie had been away, including thrashing the sharks 33 to 5 two weeks ago. They couldn't stop talking about how Mr Butkiss's plays worked and how all the extra fitness training was helping to win games. Each week they got a chance to play and nobody missed out, it was also fun and because the boys enjoyed his training and attitude they were all trying their hardest for the new coach. Bootsie was shocked and pleased to hear the team had won every game since he had been gone. He couldn't wait to start training and get back playing with the Hornets on Saturday.

He also went over and thanked Mr Butkiss for some advice that he had given Bootsie, which really helped on the camp and during the regional games.

"It's fine Bootsie," his coach said to him after Bootsie had told him about his advice about coming off the line and meeting the defence rather than waiting for them to come to him.

He also told him about the slippery ball try and how the wet ball in the detergent bucket had helped his ball handling skills and helped him score a try for his region.

"I told you I was here to help you boys and I really meant it," his coach added. "Let's go and join the other boys and get ready for the weekend's game," he said to Bootsie as they joined the main group.

The boys worked on some passing moves that all the other boys had learned since they had been away. Bootsie and Robbie told Mr Butkiss and the rest of the team that the first move he had shown them against the Cobras was now to be called the magnet move and if the word "Magnets" was shouted during a game it meant the magnet move was on.

Saturday's game felt like a whole new season had started again for Bootsie; Robbie was like a changed boy and would do anything his new coach asked him to do on the field, including not just trying a drop goal just for the sake of it. The Hornets were playing the South East Panthers who were also a pretty good team in the competition. Their colours were red, black and white. It was a really tough and bruising encounter but the Panthers were no match for the Hornets on the day, especially with two boys from the Hornets running around in blue boots. The final score was Hornets 28, Panthers 18.

At the end of the game, Bootsie said to Mr Butkiss's son Chris that he now knew how good a coach his dad really was and was sorry he had doubted him before.

"Its fine," was all that Chris replied at the time. Chris later told Bootsie that his dad had played rugby for the region when he was younger. He had gotten injured and when he couldn't play anymore he was offered a coaching job. This was at a time when the regional team was on a good winning streak and had won the regional cup for the previous three years. The coach at that time was quite old and had been a great player when he was younger. The Regional Board decided it was too risky to use the older coach for the regional shield matches as they were only played once every four years. They replaced him with Chris's dad who at the time was a lot younger but had limited experience as a coach. It caused a lot of controversy and standing down the old coach didn't go down well with the public.

The year his dad coached they lost all three matches due to a very bad run of injuries; his dad was blamed for the losses and sacked as coach. "We moved out of the region when I was very young and went to live in the southern region to get away from it all. Dad got a new job here and wanted to come back to live here with the family again. He wanted to keep coaching me in soccer, but it's not really played around here, so I said I'd play rugby instead. It was funny how rugby seemed to find him again and he really enjoyed coaching again," said Chris to Bootsie. He was utterly shocked to hear what Chris had just told him, he thought to himself that Mr Butkiss is the true hero from this season, he didn't say much but his actions did the talking for him. Bootsie thought about the southern regions motto, "Acta non verba", actions not words. It really summed up Mr Butkiss.

The Hornets along with their new coach and coaching style made it into the semifinal later that year. They were undefeated up until the semifinal game but were beaten by a much improved Cobras team, a team which had four players in blue boots playing for them that day. Bootsie went home and looked at the trophies on his desk; he had a grand final trophy, a trophy for most improved player from last year and two trophies for playing in the two regional games earlier in the year. His prized Bulldogs trophy looked tiny next to his two massive regional trophies. As he placed the trophy he had received for this season's Hornets team next to the others he thought about what he had achieved this year. He had been selected over a number of other boys, played in both games for his region *and* scored a try in one of the games.

"Not a bad effort," he thought to himself. What he didn't know at this stage was how huge next season was going to be for him. But like I've said before, that's a whole new book.....

The End.

Check out the Bootsie website
www.bootsiebooks.com

Thanks to KooGa Rugby

www.kooga.com.au

Lightning Source UK Ltd.
Milton Keynes UK
UKOW04f2300101115

262448UK00025B/374/P